I Can Sleep Alone

Written by Frank J. Mahr

Illustrated by Dawn Bourdeau Milstrey

First published by Dog Ear Publishing
4010 W. 86th Street, Ste H
Indianapolis, IN 46268
www.dogearpublishing.net

ISBN: 978-1-4575-1895-9

Printed in the United States of America

For Tyler and Lila

Thank you for keeping me company
all those sleepless nights.

When I must go to bed

I cannot sleep alone.

My eyes are filled with fright.

I shiver to the bone.

At first I hear a noise.

There's something in the hall.

Is it out to get me?

I do not know at all.

I hear a bang outside.

The ground begins to quake.

My heart beats very fast.

My knees begin to shake.

I think I see a ghost.

It's near my closet door.

I see it flying high

above the wooden floor.

Is that a monster's foot?

It's underneath my bed.

I want to scream out loud!

I want to hide my head.

When I must go to bed

I cannot sleep alone.

My eyes are filled with fright.

I shiver to the bone.

But maybe I can sleep

alone this very night.

My room is not so bad

when looked at in the light.

The things out in the hall

creating all that noise

are only Mom and Dad.

They're cleaning up my toys.

The bang I hear outside

that puts fear in my feet

is just a big old truck

that's driving down the street.

The ghost that hovers high

above my cluttered floor

is just my winter coat

upon my closet door.

The monster foot I see

beneath my lonely bed

is just my kitten's paw –

his name is Mr. Fred.

It's not that spooky here.

My room is rather neat.

There is no need to hide

under another sheet.

The scary things I fear

seem better in the light,

and now that I'm not scared

I'll sleep alone tonight.

About the Author

Frank Mahr is a husband and the father of two wonderful kids. After graduating with a bachelor's degree in accounting and attending law school at Hofstra University, he began his career working for a law firm in New York City. He currently is employed as an in-house attorney specializing in corporate and securities law. *I Can Sleep Alone* is his first published work, the idea for which came following many sleepless nights with his son who was afraid to go to bed by himself. The author hopes that *I Can Sleep Alone* can be used as a tool by other parents and caregivers to show their children that going to sleep alone does not have to be a stressful or scary experience.

CPSIA information can be obtained at www.ICGtesting.com
Printed in the USA
BVOW07s1050120815

412965BV00006B/22/P